Duck Sock Hop

by
Jane Kohuth

Illustrated by
Jane Porter

DIAL BOOKS FOR YOUNG READERS an imprint of Penguin Group (USA) Inc.

For the AGs: Elaine Dimopolous, Kirsty McKay, Sonia Miller,

Jean Stehle-Roy, and Laura Woollett, without whom I would have no books
—J.K.

For George
—J.P.

. . . .

DIAL BOOKS FOR YOUNG READERS
A division of Penguin Young Readers Group

PUBLISHED BY THE PENGUIN GROUP

Penguin Group (USA) Inc., 375 Hudson Street, New York, New York 10014, U.S.A. • Penguin Group (Canada), 90 Eglinton Avenue East, Suite 700, Toronto, Ontario M4P 2Y3, Canada (a division of Pearson Penguin Canada Inc.) • Penguin Books Ltd, 80 Strand, London WC2R 0RL, England • Penguin Ireland, 25 St Stephen's Green, Dublin 2, Ireland (a division of Penguin Books Ltd) • Penguin Group (Australia), 250 Camberwell Road, Camberwell, Victoria 3124, Australia (a division of Pearson Australia Group Pty Ltd) • Penguin Books India Pvt Ltd, 11 Community Centre, Panchsheel Park, New Delhi—110 017, India • Penguin Group (NZ), 67 Apollo Drive, Rosedale, Auckland 0632, New Zealand (a division of Pearson New Zealand Ltd) • Penguin Books (South Africa) (Pty) Ltd, 24 Sturdee Avenue, Rosebank, Johannesburg 2196, South Africa • Penguin Books Ltd, Registered Offices: 80 Strand, London WC2R 0RL, England

LIBRARY OF CONGRESS CATALOGING-IN-PUBLICATION DATA
Kohuth, Jane.
Duck sock hop/by Jane Kohuth ; illustrated by Jane Porter.
p. cm.
Summary: Ducks dance their socks off at their weekly sock-hop.
ISBN 978-0-8037-3712-9 (hardcover)
[1. Stories in rhyme. 2. Ducks—Fiction. 3. Dance—Fiction. 4. Socks—Fiction.] I. Porter, Jane, 1964 Aug. 30– ill. II. Title.
PZ8.3.K826Dts 2012   [E]—dc23
2011029969

Published in the United States by Dial Books for Young Readers,
a division of Penguin Young Readers Group
345 Hudson Street, New York, New York 10014 • www.penguin.com/youngreaders

Designed by Jason Henry
Manufactured in China • First Edition
3 5 7 9 10 8 6 4

Ducks pull socks
from a big sock box:

Socks with stripes
and socks with spots,

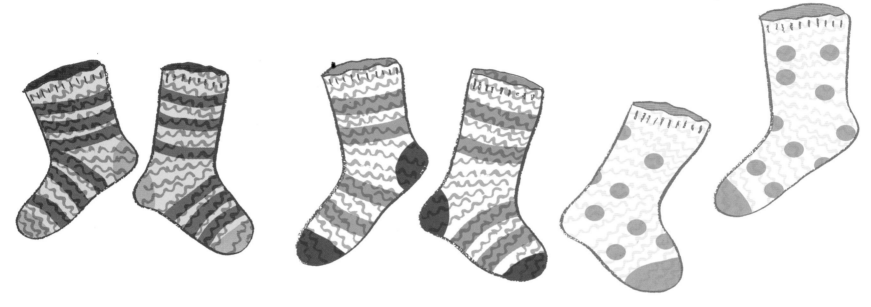

socks with squares
and socks with dots.

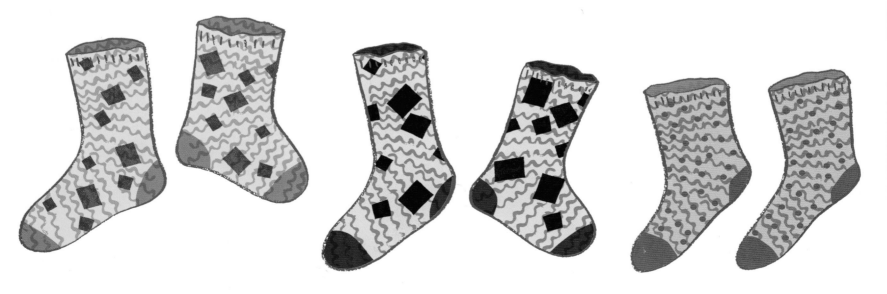

Socks with stars
and socks with moons,

socks with cars
and socks with spoons.

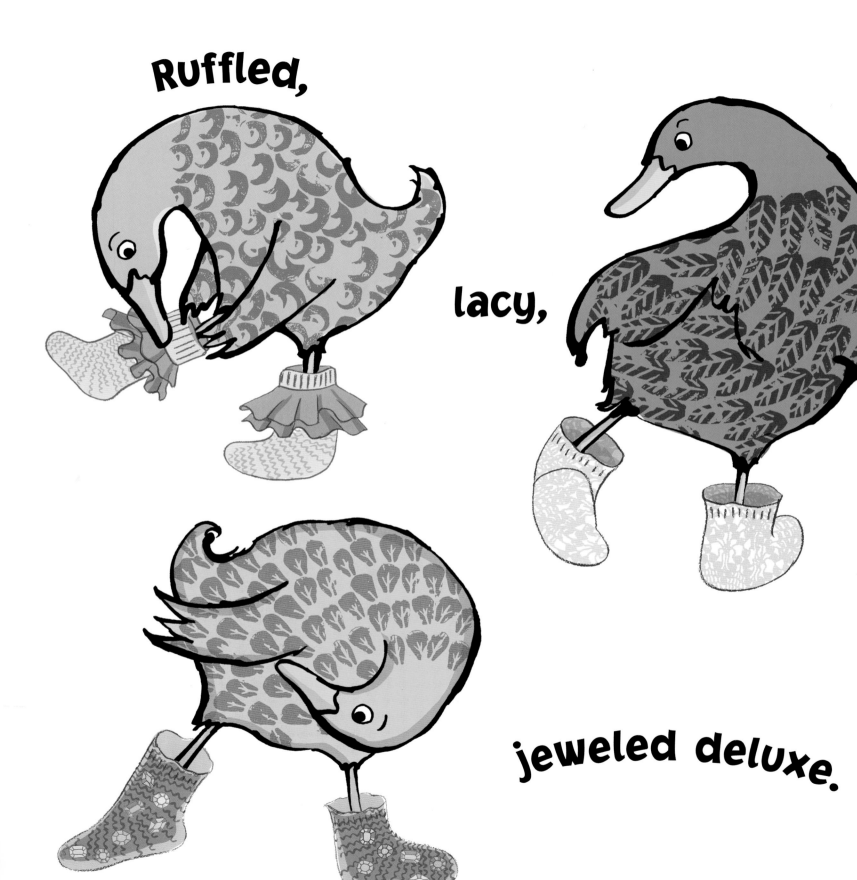

Ruffled,

lacy,

jeweled deluxe.

Left sock, right sock,

socks on ducks.

Warm up, wiggle,
stretch your beak.

Duck Sock Hop
comes once a week.

The mood is high, the sun is low,

the music starts, get ready, go!

Three ducks boogie.

One duck
rocks.

Two ducks stop and trade their socks.

Ducks line up to

dance in rows.

They kick their feet
and touch their toes.

Ducks drop crumbs,

ducks spill juice.

Socks get sticky,
socks get loose.

Holes appear in three sock heels.

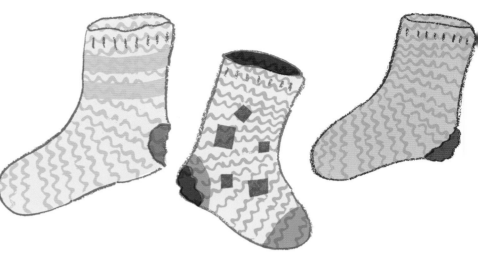

Two cars lose their button wheels.

Four jewels scatter,

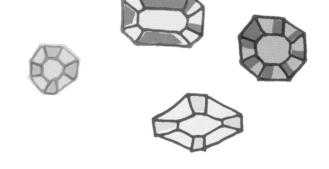

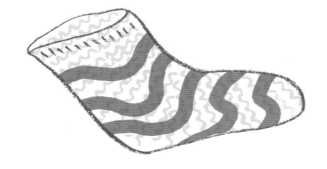

five stripes sag,

one duck's ruffles
start to drag...

Socks go STRETCH.
Socks go RIP!

Ducks teeter,
tumble,
twist,
and trip.

With a scratch, screech, BAM, the music stops,

and ducks fall down
in big duck flops!

Ducks get Band-Aids.
Ducks get snacks.

They wave good-bye
with happy quacks.

**Flocks of friends
march down the street
with empty box and bare duck feet.**

But soon enough, ducks want new socks.

They fetch their friends and grab their box.

**Then dance on down to
the Duck Sock Shop,**

and count the days
   to the next sock hop!